# The Panic Broadcast of 1938

## by Michael Druce

**Baker's Plays**
**7611 Sunset Blvd.**
**Los Angeles, CA 90042**
**BAKERSPLAYS.COM**

**THE PANIC BROADCAST OF 1938**
ISBN 978-0-87440-305-3                                      #1799-B

# CAST OF CHARACTERS

**ANDY:** Seventeen, June's boyfriend.

**SHERIFF CARTER:** A widower in his forties.

**TOM:** Early twenties.

**HANK:** Slightly older than Tom.

**LESTER:** Seventeen.

**NESTOR:** Forties, Lester's uncle.

**MARGIE CARTER:** Eighteen, out of school, daughter of the sheriff.

**JUNE GILROY:** Seventeen, still in school, Margie's best friend.

**MARLENE:** Forties, owner of the local diner, engaged to Sheriff Carter.

**MISS PARSONS:** Forties, Sunday school teacher.

**LILY GILROY:** June's younger sister.

**RAINEY:** Andy's older sister.

**JESS:** Eighteen.

**DEPUTY ELLER:** Forties.

**WIDOW O'DELL:** Sixties

**FIVE CITIZENS:** Variable ages and gender.

**MAYOR RUSHTON:** Forties, Mayor and Civil Defense Captain of Misty Valley

**CORONER:** Thirties.

**RADIO NARRATOR:** The radio voice of War of the Worlds.

Casting Note: As many extras may be added as desired. Ages for adults are suggested minimums.

# SETTING

Misty Valley Park. Misty Valley is a small town in southeast Pennsylvania. It is October 30, 1938. Left of center stands the statue of a Civil War infantryman, a pair of benches on either side. Right of center is a gazebo or a small stage. There is the suggestion of a pathway between the gazebo and the statue leading upstage. Trees and bushes fill the bare places. Perhaps old fashioned gas lamps are positioned along the path to provide light when the power in Misty Valley goes out.

# SYNOPSIS OF SCENES

Act I – Misty Valley Park – Sunday, October 30, 1938
Scene 1: A few minutes before 8 P.M.
Scene 2: Approximately twenty minutes later
Act II – Misty Valley Park - Sunday, October 30, 1938
Scene 1: Thirty minutes later
Scene 2: Approximately 9:30

## COSTUMES

Casual dress that one would expect of teenagers and adults in 1938.

## PROPS

Andy – Bicycle (optional)
Deputy Eller – Billy club
Margie – Suitcase
Tom – Lunch bag
Nestor – Double barrel shotgun
Rainey – 3 vintage gas masks
Widow O'Dell – Wrist cast
Citizens – Assorted clubs and weapons

## NOTES

The War of the Worlds broadcast on the night of October 30, 1938 set off an unexpected chain of events. Today the panic broadcast continues to excite the imagination. The full extent of the hysteria surrounding the broadcast has always been a matter of interpretation. Some historians downplay the impact of the broadcast, while others suggest it was far reaching. Taking its cue from the latter interpretation, this play is a work of a fiction that imagines what could have happened in an imaginary Pennsylvania town not far from Grover's Mill, New Jersey. There is a factual basis for some of the incidents in the play. A meteor did fall near Chicora, Pennsylvania in the summer of 1938. After the broadcast began, citizens reportedly hung wet cloths over their windows to absorb poison gas, the lights did go out in a least one town in Washington, and there was at least one report of a water tower being mistaken for a Martian tripod. Everything else is comic speculation.

## EXCERPTS FROM WAR OF THE WORLDS

Material adapted from the H.G. Wells novel *The War of the Worlds* used by permission of A P Watt Ltd on behalf of the Literary Executors of the Estate of H.G. Wells and Jeff Wayne trading as Ollie Record Productions.

# ACT I

## Scene 1

*(In the dark: we hear the sound of a radio being tuned. Since the year is 1938, it should have that crackly, tinny sound we associate with radios of that era.*

**RADIO ANNOUNCER.** The Columbia Broadcasting System and its network of affiliated stations present the Mercury Theater, starring Orson Welles in –

*(Before the program introduction is completed, we hear the radio dial being tuned to another station. We hear laughter and music. We linger a few moments on that station before switching back to the original station.)*

**RADIO NARRATOR.** No one could have believed that in the early years of this century our world was being watched keenly and closely by intelligences far greater than our own; that as we went about our daily lives, we were being observed and studied as carefully as a scientist with a microscope might observe the microscopic creatures that swim in a drop of water. No one gave a thought to the older worlds of space as sources of human danger; the idea of life upon those distant worlds seemed impossible or, at best, improbable. It is curious to recall some of the mental habits of those departed days. Even if we fancied there might be life on Mars, it would most certainly be inferior to ours; as such, we would welcome a missionary enterprise. Yet across the gulf of space, intellects vast and cool and unsympathetic, regarded this earth with envious eyes, and slowly and surely they drew their plans against us.

*(**SCENE:** The radio fades out as the lights fade up on a park in the center of Misty Valley, a small town in southeast Pennsylvania. It is October 30, 1938. Right of center is a gazebo such as the ones used for summertime concerts. Left of center stands the statue of a Civil War infantryman. A pair of park benches sits to the sides and front of the statue. There is the suggestion of a pathway crossing downstage from left to right, branching off in the space between the gazebo and statue and ambling upstage. Perhaps gas lamps light the pathway. In the background is a suggestion of trees beyond which are houses. Off-stage left is the jail and further on the train station. Off-stage right is the ice-cream parlor, Marlene's Diner, the feed store, and other businesses.)*

*(At rise: **LESTER** and **RAINEY** enter left, crossing to center stage.)*

**RAINEY.** Lester, will you slow down. I am practically out of breath. I said let's take a walk together, not a gallop.

**LESTER.** Rainey, you know how Marlene is. If she finds out I've been out walking with you when I should be making a delivery, she'll – she'll –

**RAINEY.** She'll what?

**LESTER.** Well, I don't know what, but it sure won't be very nice.

**RAINEY.** You're just a big old fraidy-cat.

**LESTER.** I am not afraid of anything. I just have a cautious respect for my boss.

**RAINEY.** Fine, I've got to get home anyway. I don't want to miss the radio.

**LESTER.** Kiss me?

**RAINEY.** You don't have time.

**LESTER.** See you tomorrow at school.

**RAINEY.** Don't forget about Sally's Halloween party tomorrow night. You are going to take me, aren't you?

**LESTER.** Unless Marlene needs me to work.

**RAINEY.** I'd rather not have to tag along with June and

Andy. Going places with my brother and his girl friend makes me feel like spare wheel.

**LESTER.** See you tomorrow.

*(Exits right.)*

**RAINEY.** Bye.

*(**LILY, JUNE,** and **MARGIE** enter left.)*

**LILY.** Hi, Rainey.

**RAINEY.** Hi, Lily. Out for a walk?

**LILY.** Daddy said I needed some fresh air.

**RAINEY.** Your mom and dad wanted some time alone, huh?

**LILY.** We walked the entire town.

**JUNE.** Lily is like a puppy on a leash. I think we walked it in record time.

**MARGIE.** Either we're getting faster or Misty Valley is getting smaller.

**LILY.** Let's do it again.

**MARGIE.** My feet are so sore you'll have to pull me in a wagon.

**JUNE.** Rainey, are you on your way home?

**RAINEY.** Can't miss Edgar Bergen.

*(Glancing at her watch.)*

Gosh, it's already started.

**LILY.** I love that show. Charlie McCarthy is so funny. Don't you just love Charlie?

**JUNE.** Would you mind walking Lily? I told Andy I'd meet him after work.

**LILY.** Do I have to?

**JUNE.** You don't want to miss the radio.

**LILY.** Someone needs to invent a gizmo that records radio programs. That way you could listen to them anytime you wanted.

**MARGIE.** Right after they invent the flying car.

**RAINEY.** Tell my brother he owes me. Come on, Lily, we better go before they start rolling up the sidewalks.

**MARGIE.** Watch out for the boogeyman.

**LILY.** Very funny.

*(To **RAINEY** as they exit up center stage)*

There is no boogeyman, is there?

**MARGIE.** Another exciting chapter in the life of Misty Valley.

*(To the statue)*

How you doing, Pete? What's the news? Any word on who's going to play Scarlet O'Hara? June and I have this bet. She thinks it will be Bette Davis. My money is on Tallulah Bankhead.

**JUNE.** Three months ago we found out Clark Gable is playing Rhett Butler. Why is it taking so long to decide?

**MARGIE.** Life magazine says they've interviewed over fourteen-hundred actresses. Of course they haven't interviewed Margie Carter.

**JUNE.** You haven't even read *Gone with the Wind*. What do you care?

*(Sound: A train whistles – not far away.)*

**MARGIE.** Hear that, Pete? No? That's alright, you're busy keeping guard. Don't forget, we're depending on you to keep Misty Valley safe from becoming too exciting.

*(To **JUNE**.)*

Pete never has been much of a talker. Can you imagine a big star like Clark Gable coming to a place like this? For that matter, can you imagine anyone coming to a place this like? The name alone is enough to keep anyone away. Instead of something like Happy Valley or Sunny Valley, the founders name it Misty Valley.

**JUNE.** Makes you wonder what they were thinking.

**MARGIE.** My theory is everyone was living in a perpetual fog that never cleared.

**JUNE.** I asked Mrs. Jenkins once. All she did was to tell me how many battles had been fought here. She said no matter where you put a foot down, you could be sure a soldier had fallen there.

**MARGIE.** That's gruesome.

**JUNE.** I know. I couldn't walk barefoot for a month.

**MARGIE.** When I was little, I had this idea that Misty Valley was named after a little girl like me.

**JUNE.** Was she a princess?

**MARGIE.** No, she was a regular person, only her name sounded like a town. Don't you think things should be named after regular people? The famous are already famous, so why make them more famous by naming something after them? How about a town called Margie Carter?

**JUNE.** What has Margie Carter done to have a town named after her?

**MARGIE.** Nothing, yet. But one of these days –

**SHERIFF.** *(Enters right.)* One of these days? What's going to happen one of these days?

**MARGIE.** Hi, Daddy. Nothing, I was just taking a flight of fancy.

**JUNE.** Hello, Mr. Carter.

**SHERIFF.** Hello, June.

(*To* **MARGIE.**)

Margie, it is too late for you and June to be out by yourselves.

**MARGIE.** We're waiting for Andy to get off work. It shouldn't be long.

**SHERIFF.** Have you done your chores?

**MARGIE.** Yes, I've slopped the pigs, fed the cattle, baled hay, swept, cooked, done the laundry, walked fifteen miles uphill each way to –

**SHERIFF.** A little less levity, please. What about Grandma?

**MARGIE.** You won't get much levity out of her.

**SHERIFF.** Have you checked in on her?

**MARGIE.** She's fine. The radio is tuned to CBS. Her hearing aid is cranked up all the way. She's as snug as a bug in a rug.

**SHERIFF.** Very well. You two be careful. You never know —

**MARGIE.** Daddy, Misty Valley is the sleepiest village in all of Pennsylvania. I don't think you have anything to worry about. Besides, old Pete will protect us.

**SHERIFF.** Usually I wouldn't be concerned, but there were a couple of break-ins over at Cantrell recently, so I do worry. The sheriff there is looking for a pair of shady characters.

**MARGIE.** If we see any shady characters, we'll scream at the top of our lungs, unless of course they're handsome.

**SHERIFF.** Nine o'clock at the latest.

**MARGIE.** Yes, Daddy.

**SHERIFF.** I should be finished with my rounds by nine, so I'll expect to see you home. Goodnight, June.

**JUNE.** Goodnight, Mr. Carter

(**SHERIFF** *exits up center stage.*)

**MARGIE.** You'd never know I am eighteen years old and out of school.

**JUNE.** Worrying is part of the job description. My mother says that's what parents are required to do. Wouldn't you rather have a daddy who worries than one who doesn't?

**MARGIE.** When your daddy is the Sheriff, worrying takes on a whole new meaning. I need to get out of this town. I need to be gone like the wind.

**JUNE.** Where would you go? What would you do?

**MARGIE.** I don't know. I haven't gotten that far in my thinking. All I know is I feel stifled here. Everyone watching you, and worrying, and knowing your business. Don't you think about getting away and seeing the real world?

**JUNE.** For me Misty Valley is the real world. I've lived here my whole life. I don't know what it's like anywhere else. Don't you think Misty Valley is probably like every place else?

**MARGIE.** I hope not. Even if it is, I need to find out. In little more than a year it will be 1940, a new decade, the future, and here we are stuck in the past. I don't want to be stuck in the past, otherwise I'll just think myself into a depression. Our first opportunity out, we should leave.

JUNE. You may not be afraid of what's out there, but I am. I don't mind admitting I'm a small town girl. I'm not ready for that, not yet.

MARGIE. What are you afraid of? The unknown? That's what makes life exciting. I can't wait. I won't miss this place one bit.

(MARLENE, *appearing anxious, enters right.*)

JUNE. Hi, Marlene.

MARLENE. Hello, June.

*(To* MARGIE.*)*

Margie, I'm looking for your daddy. Have you seen him about?

MARGIE. *(Not enthused about seeing* MARLENE.*)* He was here a few minutes ago. He's finishing up his rounds.

MARLENE. I really need to see him.

MARGIE. If it's something about the wedding –

MARLENE. It's not. It's something on the radio. It might be nothing, but if you see him again, would you ask him to stop by the diner?

MARGIE. Yes, Ma'am.

(MARLENE *exits right.*)

The radio, my foot. Of course it's something about the wedding. She has practically hounded Daddy to death about it.

JUNE. You're just nitpicking. A wedding takes a lot of plan-ning.

MARGIE. Then they should have eloped.

JUNE. You knew your daddy was bound to get married again.

MARGIE. He could have waited a bit longer.

**JUNE.** It's been two years. You're not the only one looking for happiness.

**MARGIE.** You want me to be reasonable, and I don't want to be.

**JUNE.** Margie, Marlene is making the effort, and you're not making it very easy for her.

**MARGIE.** Which is another reason I want out of here. I don't want to be any part of that wedding. It tarnishes the memory of my mother.

**JUNE.** That's not true, and you know it. Your daddy was devoted to your mother. But it's time to move on.

**MARGIE.** And that's just what I plan to do that as soon as I have the opportunity. Now, can we talk about something else?

**JUNE.** Fine. You brought it up.

*(They both fold their arms and remain silent for a moment.)*

**MARGIE.** Have you decided if you're going to Sally's Halloween party tomorrow night?

**JUNE.** It depends on how much homework I have. Lucky you.

**MARGIE.** Lucky me, all right, graduated and working at the diner for my future step-mother. I'll probably end up having to work. Whose idea was it to put Halloween on a Monday anyway?

**JUNE.** No one put it there. That's just when it is. If I do go, I'm thinking of going as Snow White or one of the Andrews sisters.

**MARGIE.** That's funny. An Andrews sister. I get it.

**JUNE.** You get what?

**MARGIE.** Andrew's girlfriend goes to a Halloween party as one of the Andrews sisters? Clever.

**JUNE.** I hadn't even thought about that.

*(**TOM** and **HANK** enter left. They are wearing caps.)*

**TOM.** Excuse us, we don't mean to interrupt.

JUNE. Oh! Hello.

HANK. We were wondering if you could tell us where we can get a bite to eat around here. Maybe a little grocery store or a diner.

(**MARGIE** *and* **JUNE** *are a little wary of these strangers.*)

MARGIE. Er. Well –

TOM. We're not from around here. My name is Tom, and this is Hank.

MARGIE. Hi, I'm Margie. This is my friend, June.

JUNE. *(Quickly.)* Margie's father is the sheriff.

TOM. Really?

JUNE. Yes, he was just here. He's coming right back, isn't he, Margie?

MARGIE. Yes, yes he is. He should be here any second.

HANK. That's good to know. Like Tom said, we're just passing through

MARGIE. You didn't come from Cantrell, did you?

HANK. Where?

JUNE. Cantrell is a little town about five miles from here.

TOM. No, we just came up from the train station.

HANK. We stopped for water.

TOM. The train stopped for water. We stopped for food.

JUNE. Trains usually don't stop here on Sunday evenings.

HANK. It's a special. We're heading to Pittsburg and points west.

TOM. It's a circus train.

JUNE. You're with the circus?

HANK. In a manner of speaking.

MARGIE. The Greatest Show on Earth?

TOM. No, that's Ringling Brothers Barnum and Bailey. Theirs is a three ring circus. Ours is more like one ring.

HANK. It's a small circus.

JUNE. Are you acrobats?

HANK. No.

MARGIE. Clowns?

TOM. No, we're handlers.

MARGIE. What's a handler?

TOM. We take care of the animals. Ours is the animal train. A couple of tigers, miniature horses, an elephant. It's a slow train.

JUNE. Where is everyone else?

HANK. They go ahead on another train. By now they're probably already in Pittsburg setting up or they're asleep.

TOM. It's just us, the engineer, the brakeman, and Jess. Jess takes care of Bonny.

JUNE. Who's Bonny?

TOM. She's the elephant.

JUNE. Oh.

MARGIE. I bet that's a great life. It sure sounds like a lot of fun. Is it fun?

TOM. It is. I mean, it's work. But you get to travel and see the country. There's a never a dull moment.

MARGIE. Really?

HANK. Well, look, it was nice to meet you. But –

TOM. We've got to get going. We pull out at ten o'clock. We told Jess we'd bring her something to eat.

MARGIE. Sure.

HANK. A place to eat? Is there anything open?

JUNE. There's a diner around the corner, next to the ice cream parlor, a place called Marlene's.

HANK. Anything you'd recommend?

MARGIE. Ask Marlene to call off the wedding.

HANK. What?

JUNE. Try the meatloaf. It's Marlene's specialty.

TOM. It was nice to meet you. Goodnight.

*(They exit right.)*

**MARGIE & JUNE.** Goodnight.

**MARGIE.** Did you hear that? Never a dull moment. My life has been one continuous dull moment, and it's all about the change. I believe I am smitten.

**JUNE.** You are not.

**MARGIE.** Oh, yes I am, because I have just found my ticket out of Misty Valley.

**JUNE.** Your daddy is not going to let you join the circus.

**MARGIE.** It won't make any difference. By the time he finds out, I'll be in Pittsburg or points west.

*(Sound: Bicycle bell.)*

*(**ANDY** enters left on a bicycle that he parks beside the gazebo.)*

**MARGIE.** Hi, Andy.

**ANDY.** Hi, Margie. Whew, that was a long ride. Have you been waiting long?

**JUNE.** Not very. Besides, we've had plenty of company.

**MARGIE.** We just met some boys from the circus train.

**JUNE.** Margie has fallen in love and is thinking of running away – tonight.

**ANDY.** Tonight? Aren't you being hasty?

**MARGIE.** Not a bit. I am tired of living in the dullest place on earth. From now on it's Margie Carter, circus girl. One day they'll name a town after me.

**ANDY.** Do you know anything about the circus?

**MARGIE.** What's to know? I'll be going from one town to the next, only the next one will be exciting. I am ready for some excitement in my life.

**JUNE.** Well, I am ready for some ice cream.

**ANDY.** You two go on. I need to go back.

**JUNE.** To O'Dell's? You just got here.

**ANDY.** You know how you sometimes get a nagging feeling there was something you forgot to do? I think I forgot to lock to gate to Bessie's stall.

**MARGIE.** Widow O'Dell's prized Holstein?

**ANDY.** I think so. If Bessie gets loose, Widow O'Dell will have a cow.

**JUNE.** She's got more cows than she knows what to do with. What's one more?

**MARGIE.** If she loses a cow, but then she has a cow, won't she be even?

**ANDY.** I better ride back down there.

**JUNE.** Don't be silly. It's too far in the dark. What's the worst that could happen?

**ANDY.** Bessie could wander up to the high road.

**MARGIE.** Isn't there one of those things that cows are afraid to step on?

**ANDY.** Yes, there's a cow guard, but Bessie is a smart cow.

**MARGIE.** Andy, cows are nice, but they are not smart. That's why there are no cows in the circus.

**ANDY.** I should check.

**MARGIE.** I'm telling you, no circus cows.

**JUNE.** Can you call Widow O'Dell?

**ANDY.** She doesn't have a phone.

**MARGIE.** It's 1938. Who doesn't have a phone?

**JUNE.** Let's get our ice cream, then we'll walk to my house, and I'll ask my daddy to drive us out to O'Dell's. I'm sure he won't mind.

**MARGIE.** Uh, oh! Here comes Miss Parsons. You know what that means. I'll catch up with you in a little bit. I've got to look in on my Grandma. If you see those circus boys again, tell them I want to talk to them.

(**MARGIE** *exits upstage as* **MISS PARSONS** *enters right.*)

**JUNE.** Hello, Miss Parsons.

**MISS PARSONS.** Good evening, June. Good evening, Andrew.

**ANDY.** Miss Parsons.

**MISS PARSONS.** Andrew, I don't believe I saw you in Sunday school this morning.

**ANDY.** No, Ma'am, you did not. I had to work today. I'm helping Widow O'Dell for a few days while she recovers from a broken wrist.

**MISS PARSONS.** I see. Well, let's pray Widow O'Dell has a speedy recovery. Young people such as you need to be in church on Sundays.

**ANDY.** Yes, Miss Parsons.

**MISS PARSONS.** I always say to myself, Neva, if the world were to end to tonight, would your soul be right? Would your soul be right, Andrew?

**ANDY.** Yes, Ma'am, I hope so.

**MISS PARSONS.** Let's not hope so, Andrew. Let's make sure. I expect to see you in Sunday school next week as well as Wednesday meeting.

**ANDY.** Yes, Ma'am.

**MISS PARSONS.** You know, June, a young lady and a young man alone and unsupervised might convey the wrong impression.

**JUNE.** Yes, Ma'am.

**MISS PARSONS.** You know how judgmental people can be.

**JUNE.** Yes, Ma'am, I do.

**MISS PARSONS.** I hope you won't be out Trick or Treating tomorrow night or attending any those Halloween parties I've been hearing about.

**JUNE.** No, Ma'am.

**MISS PARSONS.** Good. Well, I must be on my way. I have been invited to the Kohler's this evening to listen to the Chase & Sanborn Hour. Not that I endorse drinking coffee mind you, but I do love listening to that delightful Charlie McCarthy. He seems like such a sensible and wholesome young man. I bet he's in church every Sunday morning.

**JUNE.** He's a dummy.

**MISS PARSONS.** *(Shocked.)* June Gilroy, that is an awful thing to say.

**JUNE.** It's true, Charlie McCarthy is a dummy.

**MISS PARSONS.** I declare, I have never heard you speak ill of another human being.

JUNE. He isn't a human being, Miss Parsons. Everyone knows Edgar Bergen is a ventriloquist. Charlie McCarthy is just a wooden dummy.

ANDY. You did know that, didn't you?

MISS PARSONS. (*Perplexed.*) Why of course I did. I must have misunderstood you. Good night.

JUNE & ANDY. Good night, Miss Parsons.

(**MISS PARSONS** *exits upstage.*)

ANDY. Busybody.

JUNE. She means well.

ANDY. Come on, let's get that ice cream.

JUNE. (*Feeling a sudden chill.*) I think I might want hot chocolate instead.

(**LESTER** *hurries on right, agitated.*)

LESTER. Andy, June!

ANDY. Hey, Lester. What's the matter?

LESTER. Have you seen the sheriff? I've got to find Sheriff Carter. Marlene sent me to find him.

JUNE. Marlene was here a while ago. Margie told her the Sheriff is making his rounds.

ANDY. Is something wrong?

LESTER. Have you been listening to the radio?

ANDY. No, we've been here.

LESTER. Well, you should be. We've been listening to it at the diner. There's some really weird stuff going on. A fireball fell out of the sky onto a farm in Grover's Mill.

JUNE. Grover's Mill?

ANDY. Isn't that in New Jersey?

LESTER. Near Trenton, less than a hundred miles from here.

ANDY. Was anyone hurt?

LESTER. I don't know. It's a special report.

JUNE. It's probably a meteorite, like the one that fell on Chicora during the summer.

**LESTER.** It's not a meteor. It's a cylinder.

**ANDY.** A cylinder?

**LESTER.** That's what they're reporting on the radio.

**ANDY.** If it is, then it's probably something that fell off an airplane.

**LESTER.** No, they're saying it's something that came from space. They're talking about seeing explosions on Mars and rockets heading toward Earth.

**ANDY.** It's got to be some sort of joke.

**JUNE.** Lester, you can't always believe the radio. They just make up stuff to keep people listening.

**LESTER.** I don't think so. We were all listening to the Chase & Sanborn Hour. You know how Edgar Bergen always takes a break at ten minutes after the hour, Marlene tunes in to CBS for a few minutes, and there it was, a special report.

**ANDY.** The news is on CBS, but not on NBC? There's nothing about it on the Edgar Bergen show?

**LESTER.** Not a thing.

**JUNE.** That doesn't make sense.

**LESTER.** Maybe NBC doesn't know.

**ANDY.** How could they not know? Their studios are practically next door to each other.

**LESTER.** They're not broadcasting from New York. They're broadcasting live from Grover's Mill.

**ANDY.** Lester, have you been into your uncle's moonshine?

**LESTER.** No, I have not – hey, how do you know about that?

**ANDY.** Oh, come on, Lester. Everybody knows about Nestor's still. When was the last time anyone kept a secret in this town?

(**TOM** *and* **HANK** *enter right.*)

**LESTER.** Those two guys were in the diner, they'll tell you.

(*To* **TOM** *and* **HANK.**)

Hey, you fellers were in the diner. You heard the news report about the fireball landing in New Jersey.

ANDY. Is he telling the biggest Halloween joke anybody
    ever heard?

HANK. No, it's definitely on the radio.

TOM. Something about a big metal object.

HANK. If it is joke, it sure sounds real.

LESTER. It isn't a joke.

JUNE. I agree with Andy, I think it's just a Halloween prank.

    *(To* TOM *and* HANK.*)*

    Did you get some food?

TOM. *(Holding up a bag.)* The meatloaf.

JUNE. *(Realizing she hasn't introduced* ANDY.*)* This is my
    – Andy.

TOM. *(To* ANDY.*)* Pleased to meet you. This is my buddy
    Hank.

    *(To* JUNE.*)*

    Is your friend still around?

JUNE. Margie? She went to look in on her Grandma. She
    said if we saw you to tell you she wants to talk to you.

TOM. I guess we can spare a few minutes.

SHERIFF. *(Enters center.)* That's good.

LESTER. Sheriff, thank goodness. Have you been listening
    to the radio?

SHERIFF. No, Lester, I've been making my rounds.

LESTER. You need to come down to the diner right away.

SHERIFF. Give me just a couple of minutes, Lester.

    *(To* TOM *and* HANK.*)*

    You fellers are not from around here.

HANK. No, sir. We arrived a while ago on the train. We just
    stopped to get a bite to eat.

SHERIFF. On a Sunday night?

HANK. It's a special.

TOM. It's a circus train.

SHERIFF. I see. You have some identification?

**HANK.** Have we done something wrong, Sheriff?

**SHERIFF.** I don't know. That's why I have some questions for you. When was the last time you were in Cantrell?

**TOM.** I – I don't think we've ever been to Cantrell.

*(To* **HANK.***)*

Have we?

**HANK.** I haven't.

**SHERIFF.** If you had, you might not want to admit that.

**MARGIE.** *(Enters center.)* Daddy, what are you doing?

**SHERIFF.** Margie, this is none of your business. You need to head home.

**MARGIE.** You said I could stay out until nine o'clock. It's not even eight-thirty yet.

**SHERIFF.** I said head home.

**MARGIE.** I've been home. Grandma's listening to that crazy program about fireballs dropping out of the sky. It's too weird for me.

**LESTER.** Sheriff, that's what Marlene sent me to talk to you about.

**SHERIFF.** Hold on, Lester. I'm not finished with these two.

*(To* **TOM** *and* **HANK.***)*

What did you say your names are?

**HANK.** We didn't.

**MARGIE.** This is Tom and this is Hank.

**SHERIFF.** You know these boys?

**MARGIE.** We met them right after you told me I could stay out till nine. Tell him June.

**JUNE.** They said they were from the circus train and they were looking for something to eat.

**TOM.** *(Holding up the bag.)* Meatloaf.

**HANK.** Sheriff, if we've done something wrong –

**MARGIE.** You haven't done anything wrong.

**SHERIFF.** Margie, you keep out of this.

*(To* **TOM** *and* **HANK.***)*

In the last couple of weeks, there have been some break-ins over at Cantrell, and you two match the description: between the ages of twenty and sixty, one-hundred to two-hundred pounds, five to six feet tall.

**MARGIE.** Daddy!

**SHERIFF.** What did I say?

**HANK.** That description could fit anyone.

*(Pointing to **LESTER**.)*

Even him.

**LESTER.** Me? I'm not a burglar.

**SHERIFF.** Lester, no one is accusing you anything.

**LESTER.** Sheriff, if you don't come now, Marlene will serve my head on a platter.

**MARGIE.** *(To **TOM**.)* That's where Marlene gets her meatloaf.

**SHERIFF.** Margie, you are not helping things here.

*(To **LESTER**.)*

Lester, you tell Marlene –

**LESTER.** Sheriff Carter, in all due respect, I cannot tell Marlene anything. She's your fiancée. When she says she wants to see you, well, that's who she wants to see. I can't go back without you.

**MARGIE.** *(To **SHERIFF**)* Serves you right.

**SHERIFF.** Margie, hush.

*(To **TOM** and **HANK**.)*

I'm not finished with you fellers. So I'm going to park you in the jail house for a short time and then I'll be right back.

**HANK.** You're locking us up?

**SHERIFF.** Let's just call it protective custody.

**TOM.** Our train leaves at ten o'clock.

**SHERIFF.** And if everything checks out, you'll be on it. You'll be in the capable hands of Deputy Eller.

**MARGIE.** You're arresting them?

**SHERIFF.** Margie, this is none of your business.

**MARGIE.** Tom, I am so sorry. Is there room for me on that train?

**TOM.** *(Not sure how to answer.)* Well – I – suppose so.

**SHERIFF.** Have you taken leave of your senses? Margie Carter, you go home immediately.

**MARGIE.** I will not. I am eighteen years old, and I will do as I please.

**SHERIFF.** Fine, stay.

**MARGIE.** No! I am going home.

**SHERIFF.** We'll talk about this later.

*(To **LESTER.**)*

Lester, go on back to the diner. Tell Marlene I'll be along shortly.

*(Exits left with **HANK** and **TOM.**)*

**LESTER.** I'm a dead man.

*(Exits right.)*

**MARGIE.** I have never been so embarrassed in all of my life.

**JUNE.** He's just doing his job.

**MARGIE.** Why do you keep defending him? I am going home to pack a suitcase.

*(**MARGIE** exits up center.)*

**ANDY.** It's not even a full moon.

**JUNE.** *(Looking up into the sky as **ANDY** stares at her.)* Still, it is beautiful, isn't it?

**ANDY.** Yes.

**JUNE.** You'd think with all those millions of stars –

**ANDY.** Professor Ogden says there's less than a one in a million chance.

**JUNE.** Then the odds are pretty good that there's at least one.

**ANDY.** And here we are. Can I kiss you?

JUNE. *(A gentle admonishment.)* Andy.

ANDY. You can't blame a guy for asking.

JUNE. Come on, let's get over to the soda shop before it closes.

(**ANDY** *and* **JUNE** *exit right.*)

## Scene 2

*(In the dark: We hear another snippet from the radio broadcast.)*

**RADIO ANNOUNCER.** The top of the cylinder is twisting off. Something is moving in the shadows. It's – it's coming out. There's one, no, two luminous disks that look like eyes. Now, something resembling a snake. No, not a snake. They're tentacles. It's rising. It's coming out. It's coming toward us.

*(**SCENE::** It is approximately ten minutes later. As the broadcast fades, the lights fade up. Nestor enters from up center as Lester rushes on breathlessly from stage right.)*

**LESTER.** Uncle Nestor, have you seen Andy and June?

**NESTOR.** I haven't been looking for them. I've been too busy packing my gear.

**LESTER.** Have you been listening to the radio?

**NESTOR.** Lester, I've heard all I need to hear. I'm heading for the hills to guard my still. I don't plan on being here when those creatures from Mars arrive. They mess with me and they'll be staring down the neck of a double barrel shotgun. Tell your granddaddy if I make it back alive, I'll bring him a gallon of my finest moonshine. Wish me luck, Lester.

*(Exits left.)*

*(**ANDY** and **JUNE** enter right.)*

**LESTER.** Andy, June, we've got to get out of here now.

**ANDY.** Whoa, whoa! Calm down. What's going on?

**LESTER.** We've been invaded.

**ANDY.** We have?

**JUNE.** We're at war?

**ANDY.** Is it the Germans? It is, isn't it? I knew it.

**LESTER.** It's the Martians.

**JUNE & ANDY.** Who?

**LESTER.** The Martians.

JUNE. Who are the Martians?

LESTER. From the planet Mars, those Martians. Remember that cylinder I told you about? It was filled with Martians. They've landed.

(*LILY rushes on from upstage center.*)

LILY. June, June! Hurry, you've got to come home at once.

JUNE. Lily, what on Earth? I thought I sent you home with Rainey.

LILY. Mom and Daddy said you've got to come home now.

JUNE. I'll be along in a few minutes.

LILY. There's no time, we're being invaded by Martians.

ANDY. Not you, too.

LESTER. The secretary of defense is declaring a national emergency and calling up the army.

ANDY. I don't believe it.

JUNE. Has anyone called the governor?

LESTER. All the phone lines are jammed. There's panic everywhere.

LILY. June, hurry. Right now they're in New Jersey.

(*To* LESTER.)

Do you think they'll cross the state line?

LESTER. They're Martians. They've traveled a million miles. Why wouldn't they?

LILY. But why would they attack Misty Valley?

LESTER. I don't know. Why would they attack Grover's Mill?

LILY. June, come on. Daddy says those things are spreading poison gas. He and Mama are putting wet cloths on the windows to keep the gas out. We've got to protect ourselves.

JUNE. I haven't heard anything, I haven't seen anything.

LESTER. That's because they're too far away right now, but they'll be here any time. There are cylinders dropping all over the East Coast. I wouldn't be surprised if that thing that dropped on Chicora in June was one of them. They're just waiting to come out and attack us. With Grover's Mill to the east of us and Chicora to the west, we're trapped in the middle.

ANDY. Lester, stop it. You're scaring Lily.

LILY. I'm already scared.

*(Several* CITIZENS *run on.)*

CITIZEN ONE. You kids shouldn't be out here. Haven't you heard? There's a Martian invasion underway. We're heading for the hills.

LILY. *(To* JUNE *and* ANDY.*)* See, what did I tell you?

LESTER. I'm heading home.

JUNE. Lester, take Lily home, will you!

LILY. June!

JUNE. It's alright, tell Mama and Daddy I'll be there in a few minutes.

*(*LESTER *and* LILY *exit right.)*

CITIZEN TWO. Grab your guns.

CITIZEN THREE. What good will guns do?

CITIZEN TWO. I don't know, but I'm not going down without a fight.

CITIZEN FOUR. I'm heading for the caves.

CITIZEN FIVE. You kids should go too. Head for the caves. Save yourselves. Save mankind. We need people to preserve the species.

*(The* CITIZENS *exit, leaving* JUNE *and* ANDY *alone.)*

JUNE. These people are scaring me.

ANDY. June, will you kiss me now?

JUNE. At a time like this?

ANDY. Especially at a time like this.

JUNE. What kind of girl do you think I am?

ANDY. I think you're the most wonderful girl in the entire world. I'm in love with you and one day I want to marry you. But right now all I want to do is kiss you. I'm afraid if we don't do it now, we may never have a chance.

(**RAINEY** *enters left, wearing a gas mask and carrying two more.*)

**JUNE.** *(Screams.)*

**RAINEY.** It's all right, it's me.

*(Pulling up her mask to show her face.)*

**ANDY.** Rainey, you half scared us to death.

**RAINEY.** I've been looking all over for you. Mom and Dad are crazy with worry.

**ANDY.** I'm fine, Rainey.

**RAINEY.** Daddy said for you and June to put one of these on. The Martians are spreading poison gas.

**ANDY.** We've heard. Rainey, there is no gas.

**RAINEY.** Not yet, but there will be. Come on, we're meeting at Aunt Mary's in about fifteen minutes.

**ANDY.** Then what?

**RAINEY.** We've packed the Studebaker and we're heading west. Put those things on.

(**JUNE** *and* **ANDY** *make a clumsy attempt to put on the masks.*)

**RAINEY.** What are you waiting for? Let's go.

**ANDY.** I need to walk June home.

**RAINEY.** How can you be so calm? Fifteen minutes, we're leaving in fifteen minutes.

*(Exits upstage center.)*

**ANDY.** I'll be there.

(**ANDY** *presses his gas mask against* **JUNE'S** *as if a clumsy attempt to kiss her.*)

**ANDY.** This is ridiculous. I'm taking this thing off

*(Pulls off gas mask.).*

**JUNE.** What about the gas?

(**JUNE** *pulls off her gas mask.*)

**ANDY.** It's just a load of hot air.

(**MARGIE** *enters right, carrying a small suitcase.*)

**MARGIE.** (*Noticing the gas masks* **JUNE** *and* **ANDY** *are holding.*) Oh, great. Don't tell me you two believe this silliness.

**JUNE.** You don't think it's true?

**MARGIE.** My Grandma has been listening to it, but then her hearing aid battery conked out, so I tuned the radio back to Edgar Bergen. They're not reporting anything.

**ANDY.** You think it's just a radio program?

**MARGIE.** It has to be. There's no such thing as people from Mars, is there?

(**JESS** *enters behind* **MARGIE.**)

**JESS.** Excuse me.

**MARGIE.** (*Screams.*)

**JESS.** I'm sorry, I didn't mean to scare you, but I'm looking for two guys. They're young, about this tall, wearing caps.

**MARGIE.** Tom and Hank?

**JESS.** You know them?

**MARGIE.** We just met.

**JESS.** Do you know where they are?

**MARGIE.** In jail.

**JESS.** Jail? What are they doing there? Are you sure?

**MARGIE.** I ought to know, my daddy is the Sheriff. I bet you're Jess, aren't you?

**JESS.** Yes. How do you know?

**MARGIE.** Tom told me. I'm Margie.

**JESS.** Why are they in jail?

**MARGIE.** Because they looked suspicious.

**JESS.** Shoot! Those boys have got to be on that train by ten o'clock. Can I talk to the Sheriff?

**MARGIE.** With all these crazy Mars rumors spreading like wild fire, he's not thinking about them. There's no way they'll be out tonight.

JESS. What do you mean Mars rumors?

MARGIE. The radio is reporting the Earth has been invaded by men from Mars. You haven't seen any weird looking people around, have you?

JESS. I work in the circus. It's filled with weirdoes. Can you get me a key to the jail?

MARGIE. My daddy has one key and his deputy has the other, and there's no way they're going to give them up.

JESS. Is there any way I can see them?

MARGIE. Not this late. The jailhouse is locked.

JESS. There's got to be some way I can talk to them. I can't manage those animals myself. Tom and Hank have got to be on that train.

MARGIE. The cell has a little window in the back that looks out onto an alley.

JESS. Can they squeeze through it?

MARGIE. No, it has bars.

ANDY. If they can't make it, what are you going to do?

JESS. I guess I'll have to go with Plan B.

MARGIE. What's Plan B?

JESS. It's probably just as well you don't know.

MARGIE. Good luck.

> (*Gingerly.*)

> Jess?

JESS. Yes?

MARGIE. Just one more thing. Are you and Tom? Well, you know —

JESS. Tom and I are just friends. It's Hank I'm sweet on, only he doesn't even know I exist. But I guess it doesn't make much difference. I've got my hands full trying to keep up with an elephant, much less trying to corral a boyfriend. See you. (*Exits.*)

MARGIE. It's Hank she's sweet on. Pittsburg, here I come.

JUNE. You really are going to leave?

**MARGIE.** On the ten o'clock train. Keep your fingers crossed I don't run into my daddy before then. I need to hide out for a while.

(*Lights flicker and then go out.* **JUNE,** **ANDY,** *and* **MARGIE** *should still be visible to the audience.*)

**JUNE.** Now what?

**ANDY.** All the power just went off.

**MARGIE.** You don't think it's the Martian's do you?

**JUNE.** I didn't think you believed in Martians.

**MARGIE.** Well, there's something going on. It just better not interfere with my plans to leave.

(*Sound: In the distance two shotgun blasts can be heard. All three look at each other.*)

**ANDY.** This is getting serious

(*Lights fade.*)

## END OF ACT I

# ACT II

## Scene 1

*(It is now thirty minutes later.)*

**RADIO ANNOUNCER.** This intense heat is projected in a parallel beam against any object they choose, by means of a polished parabolic mirror, much as the mirror of a lighthouse projects a beam of light. This thing I saw. How can I describe it? It's a monstrous tripod higher than a house, striding over the tops of trees.

*(Lights fade up, but not quite as bright as previous levels to suggest some light has been restored by way of generators.* **SHERIFF** *and* **MARLENE** *enter right.* **MAYOR RUSHTON** *enters left.)*

**MAYOR.** Sheriff, have you heard the latest? They've got heat rays and they're traveling around in metal tripods taller than trees. The army and the National Guard are powerless to stop them. We need an evacuation plan.

**SHERIFF.** Yes, we do. As mayor, you're in charge of Civil Defense. So, what is the plan?

**MAYOR.** That's why I'm asking you. We don't have a plan. We have a plan to write a plan, but we don't have a plan.

**MARLENE.** Rushton, I should never have voted for you.

**MAYOR.** Marlene Gibbons, it is not easy running this town. If you think you can do better, you are welcome to run against me next election.

**MARLENE.** If we are not wiped off the face of the planet, you bet I will.

**SHERIFF.** You two stop squabbling. We need to be working together, not against each other. There's no telling how long those emergency generators will last. Marlene, there's an old short wave radio in my basement. I need you to find it and set it up in the diner. Get Lester to help you.

**MARLENE.** If I can find him. You take care.

**SHERIFF.** I will. We'll be all right.

(**MARLENE** *exits right*)

Rushton, I need you to get some folks together and go from business to business gathering up supplies. Food, medical, you name it. Take everything to the courthouse. We've got to have a central location.

**MAYOR.** A lot of good that'll do. The courthouse will probably be mashed flatter than a pancake in no time. Then what?

(**MAYOR** *exits upstage center.*)

**SHERIFF.** It hasn't happened yet, let's try to be positive.

(**NESTOR** *enters left carrying a shotgun.*)

**NESTOR.** Sheriff, Sheriff.

**SHERIFF.** Nestor, I heard you went to the hills.

**NESTOR.** I tried, but I got waylaid out on the high road. I saw one, I tell you. I saw it with my own two eyes. It was the ugliest thing I have ever seen.

**SHERIFF.** Calm down. Draw a breath. Now, tell me, what did you see?

**NESTOR.** A Martian.

**SHERIFF.** *(Skeptically.)* Nestor.

**NESTOR.** I was on my way to check on my still.

**SHERIFF.** Now you're sure you were on your way there and not on your way back.

**NESTOR.** I was on my way there. I was listening to that report on my car radio. When I made the turn up there by O'Dell's place, there was one standing right in the middle of the road. Its eyes were glowing in the reflection of my headlights. I swerved to miss it and drove right off the road. I'm surprised I wasn't killed.

**SHERIFF.** Near Widow O'Dell's place you say?

**NESTOR.** Yes sir, right up there by the curve.

**SHERIFF.** What happened to the Martian?

**NESTOR.** *(Patting his rifle.)* I introduced it to my good buddy, Buck Shot.

**SHERIFF.** Did you kill it?

**NESTOR.** I hope so.

**SHERIFF.** You didn't check?

**NESTOR.** Of course I didn't check. The news is talking about poison gas and heat rays. I wasn't sticking around to be gassed and barbecued.

**SHERIFF.** Alright, if I have time, I'll check it out. Where can I find you, if I need you?

**NESTOR.** On the next train out of here.

*(Exits.)*

**SHERIFF.** That's the circus train. That'd be about right.

*(Exits up center.)*

*(For a moment, the stage is clear. **TOM** and **HANK** come out of the bushes. They have been hiding.)*

**HANK.** The sooner we get out this place the better. This town is loony.

**TOM.** It's making the circus look pretty respectable.

**HANK.** Do you think we can take a chance on heading back down to the station?

**TOM.** I don't know. If that deputy is looking for us, that's where she'll be.

*(Looks at his watch.)*

We've got a while yet.

**HANK.** We can't wait too long. Jess will be worried.

**TOM.** She's a tough cookie. She'll be okay

**HANK.** Shush, someone is coming

*(They duck back into the bushes.)*

*(**MARGIE** enters, carrying her suitcase. **TOM** and **HANK** pop up from behind the bushes.)*

**TOM.** Margie.

**MARGIE.** *(Gasps.)* Tom! Hank! Oh, my gosh! You scared me. What are you doing out of jail? Did my daddy let you out?

**TOM.** No, we had some help.

**HANK.** What is all this stuff about Martians?

**MARGIE.** It's that radio program. Now they're saying Mars has invaded. They are talking about monsters on stilts, heat rays, and poison gas.

**TOM.** Do you believe it?

**MARGIE.** Part of me says no, but you look around and everyone has gone crazy. You start thinking maybe you should be going crazy as well.

**HANK.** Tom, we better get moving.

**MARGIE.** Take me with you. Please.

**TOM.** But your daddy's the sheriff.

**MARGIE.** I'm eighteen and I can do whatever I want.

**TOM.** But we hardly know each other.

**MARGIE.** If the world really is coming to an end, does that really make a lot of difference?

**HANK.** She has a point.

**TOM.** All right. Are you ready?

**MARGIE.** My suitcase is packed.

**TOM.** Are you sure? Once we get on that train, we can't stop

**MARGIE.** *(A sudden crack in her determination.)* I forgot to leave a note. I need to leave a note. It won't take me long.

**TOM.** Meet us at the station.

**MARGIE.** Don't leave without me. I'll be there. *(Exiting.)*

**HANK.** Her daddy isn't going to be very happy with you.

**TOM.** He's not going to be happy anyway. Not after he sees what's left of his jail cell.

*(Sound: Two shotgun rounds are fired in the distance.)*

**HANK.** That sounds like that came from the direction of the station. We better find a place to lay low. *(They exit up center.)*

(*The* **SHERIFF** *enters left. A moment later* **DEPUTY ELLER** *comes on.*)

**DEPUTY ELLER.** Sheriff, I've been looking everywhere for you.

**SHERIFF.** You found me. Wherever those gunshots are coming from, I need you to find out.

**DEPUTY ELLER.** There's something more pressing than that. The prisoners have escaped.

**SHERIFF.** Wonderful. Just what I wanted to hear.

**DEPUTY ELLER.** I went down to my Momma's house to catch up on the news, and when I got back, they were gone. They plumb busted out.

**SHERIFF.** How is that possible?

**DEPUTY ELLER.** Well, it's like this –

**SHERIFF.** They jimmy the lock?

**DEPUTY ELLER.** No, sir.

**SHERIFF.** Did they get a hold of your key?

**DEPUTY ELLER.** No, sir.

**SHERIFF.** Exactly how did they get out?

**DEPUTY ELLER.** The entire back wall of the cell is gone. It's smashed completely down.

**SHERIFF.** I had a bad feeling about those boys.

**DEPUTY ELLER.** You think they were the ones who did those jobs over in Cantrell, but I don't think so.

**SHERIFF.** Really?

**DEPUTY ELLER.** No, sir. I think those boys are Martians.

**SHERIFF.** Martians? Eller, what makes you think that?

**DEPUTY ELLER.** Well, the whole wall is down. I don't think they could have done that on their own. I think they must have some sort of atomic communicator and they called in that Heat Ray. It blasted right through that wall. They've got weapons so advanced they can cut right through anything without leaving any burn marks. I'm scared, Sheriff.

**SHERIFF.** I don't know what Martians look like, but those boys looked pretty normal to me.

**DEPUTY ELLER.** That's what's so insidious. They can take on human form and move among us.

**SHERIFF.** I didn't know that.

**DEPUTY ELLER.** I've read about stuff like that in science fiction stories. Was it *The Time Machine* or *The Invisible Man?* Maybe it was that other one H.G. Wells wrote. What was the name of that story? On second thought, maybe it was Jules Verne.

**SHERIFF.** Eller, I don't have time for this.

**DEPUTY ELLER.** There is one other thing.

**SHERIFF.** Go on.

**DEPUTY ELLER.** There was a fatality.

**SHERIFF.** Someone was killed in the break out? One of those boys?

**DEPUTY ELLER.** No, sir, I think it must have been someone else. An innocent bystander in the alley when the wall came down.

**SHERIFF.** Could you identify who it was?

**DEPUTY ELLER.** No, sir, there was hardly anything left of them. Whatever that weapon is, it plumb turned that poor soul to mush. It just ground them up something awful.

**SHERIFF.** I'll try to get the coroner to take a look. You haven't mentioned this to anyone else, have you?

**DEPUTY ELLER.** I might have said something to the Mayor. He was on his way to secure supplies.

**SHERIFF.** I know. I sent him on that errand. Was there anyone else you might have mentioned this to?

**DEPUTY ELLER.** Well, not specifically.

**SHERIFF.** But there was someone else, wasn't there?

**DEPUTY ELLER.** Miss Parsons came upon us while I was speaking with the mayor.

**SHERIFF.** Give it thirty minutes and it'll be all over town. Can we try to keep this to ourselves?

**DEPUTY ELLER.** People need to know.

**SHERIFF.** Our job is to protect people, not scare them. We need to keep a lid on this.

**DEPUTY ELLER.** I don't know if I can do that.

**SHERIFF.** Why don't you try, otherwise you'll start a full scale panic.

**DEPUTY ELLER.** At first I thought this was a battle to save Misty Valley, but now I see it is a war to save the world.

*(A thought enters her head, but quickly disappears.)*

Sheriff, I need a gun.

**SHERIFF.** I don't think so. You go on over and see if you can find the coroner. Tell him I'll check with him shortly.

**DEPUTY ELLER.** Will do. *(Exits up center.)*

*(The* **MAYOR** *and* **MISS PARSONS** *enter left.)*

**MAYOR.** Sheriff Carter, is it true?

**SHERIFF.** Is what true, Mayor?

**MAYOR.** That you had two Martians in your jail and you let them escape.

**SHERIFF.** Did I say thirty minutes? I meant five.

**MAYOR.** What?

**SHERIFF.** Nothing. Nobody let anyone escape. Somehow they broke down the wall.

**MISS PARSONS.** This is surely the end of times. The beast has reared its head.

**SHERIFF.** The prisoners were normal looking boys. They are not Martians.

**MISS PARSONS.** And the beast may come in many disguises.

**SHERIFF.** Miss Parsons, there is no beast.

**MAYOR.** You should issue a shoot-to-kill order immediately.

**SHERIFF.** I am not going to do that. I thought I gave you job to do.

**MAYOR.** Don't forget, I am still the mayor of this town.

**SHERIFF.** Unless you want me to handcuff you to one of these benches, I suggest you do what you were told to do. I have other business to attend to.

**MISS PARSONS.** Turn the other cheek, Mayor, just turn the other cheek.

*(All three exit up center.)*

*(***JESS*** enters left, soaking wet. A moment later **MARGIE** enters with her suitcase.)*

**MARGIE.** My goodness, Jess, what happened to you? You're drenched.

**JESS.** Something bad has happened. Bonny has broken free.

**MARGIE.** The elephant?

*(***JESS*** nods.)*

How? What happened?

**JESS.** She got scared and ran off. I was exercising her when some crazy man showed up with a shotgun and started shooting at the water tower. He was yelling, "Take that you Martian devil." The entire train station is flooded.

**MARGIE.** You'll catch your death in those wet clothes. My house in nearby, I have some clothes you can change into.

**JESS.** I've got to find Bonny.

**MARGIE.** We'll find her. In a town this small, you can't hide a secret, much less an elephant.

*(**MARGIE** and **JESS** exit.)*

**END OF SCENE**

## Scene 2

*(In the blackout:)*

**RADIO ANNOUNCER.** I am filled with indescribable terror to think how quickly this desolating change has come. All about me are blackened trees, blackened, desolate ruins. Over all is – silence. I am all alone. Has mankind has been swept out of existence? Am I the last man left alive?

*(It is approximately 9:30 PM. As the lights fade up,* **HANK** *and* **TOM** *enter from up center.)*

**TOM.** It looks clear.

**HANK.** Do you think it's safe to head down to the station?

**TOM.** We'll find some bushes a few yards down the track. When the train pulls out, we'll jump aboard.

**HANK.** What about Margie?

**TOM.** If she shows up, I'll try to signal her.

*(Sound: Offstage the voice of the* **MAYOR** *is heard on a megaphone.)*

**MAYOR.** *(Offstage.)* Attention, attention. Citizens of Misty Valley, this is your Mayor. Meet in the park as soon as possible. I repeat, if you can hear me, meet in Misty Valley park.

**HANK.** We better get out of here.

*(***DEPUTY ELLER*** enters, waving her billy club.)*

**DEPUTY ELLER.** Hold it right there, Mars Boys.

**TOM.** Uh-oh.

**HANK.** What did you call us?

**DEPUTY ELLER.** Mars Boys. How dumb do you think I am?

*(***HANK*** and ***TOM*** glance at each other and shrug.)*

**DEPUTY ELLER.** You don't think I know you're Martians?

**TOM.** I don't think *we* know we're Martians.

**DEPUTY ELLER.** Don't try to play cute with me. I know you called in your heat ray to destroy that wall, and that you can change yourselves into any shape you want.

HANK. Deputy, we're not Martians. We're just two circus boys who want to get out of this town.

DEPUTY ELLER. I wouldn't expect you to confess it. But there's no way you two could have torn down that wall.

HANK. Actually, there's a pretty simple explanation for that.

DEPUTY ELLER. I know there is. You boys are aliens.

TOM. Deputy, if what you're saying is true, shouldn't you be worried? All you've got to defend yourself is a Billy club.

DEPUTY ELLER. And I'm not afraid to use it. Now, you two turn around and head on back to the jailhouse. I have a nice basement waiting for you two.

(**TOM**, *suddenly changes his voice into something other worldly sounding.*)

TOM. You are right, Deputy, we are from another world. We are here to conquer your planet. Soon, we shall be masters of the universe.

(*To* **HANK.**)

Begin the transformation process.

HANK. Huh?

TOM. (*Winking at* **HANK.**) I said, begin the transformation process.

(**HANK** *follows* **TOM'S** *lead. Both shake and distort their bodies and begin making weird sounds. Horrified,* **DEPUTY ELLER** *faints, falling behind one of the benches.* **TOM** *and* **HANK** *burst out laughing.*)

TOM. Do you think she's alright?

HANK. I think she just fainted.

TOM. Should we do something? Tell someone? Find a doctor?

HANK. She'll be alright. I'm just afraid if she wakes up and we're still here, she'll sure enough try to take us to jail. We better stay low.

**TOM.** These people have got Martians on the brain.

> *(SOUND: All of a sudden, a rustling noise is heard, as if something monstrous is crashing through the trees.* **TOM** *and* **HANK** *look at each other and run off stage left.)*

> *(***MARGIE** *and* **JESS** *enter right.* **JESS** *is transformed, wearing one of* **MARGIE'S** *dresses.)*

**JESS.** Thank you, Margie, I really appreciate you helping me out.

**MARGIE.** It was nothing. You would have done the same for me.

**JESS.** I don't often get to dress up pretty-like and look like a girl. Not traveling with the circus.

**MARGIE.** Sure, but like you say, you get to travel and see the country. It's not like being stuck in a place like this.

**JESS.** Moving from place to place gets old. There's something to be said for a place like this.

**MARGIE.** Not much.

**JESS.** You've got family and friends. Your roots are here.

**MARGIE.** It's just me and my daddy and my grandma.

**JESS.** That's more than I've got. I don't have family, unless you consider circus folk family.

**MARLENE.** *(Offstage right.)* Margie.

**MARGIE.** Shoot. It's my daddy's fiancé.

> *(***MARLENE** *enters right.)*

**MARLENE.** Margie, your daddy has been looking all over for you.

**MARGIE.** I haven't been lost.

**MARLENE.** With everything that's been going on, we've been worried.

**MARGIE.** You mean my Daddy's been worried.

**MARLENE.** Both of us have been worried.

**MARGIE.** You needn't be concerned.

**MARLENE.** But I am.

**MARGIE.** Don't be. You're not my mother.

MARLENE. That's right, Margie, I'm not. I would never try to take her place. I could never do that. I just hope I can be as good a woman as she was.

MARGIE. Jess, this is Marlene, my daddy's –

*(From under the bench we hear a groan. All three turn in shock to see* ELLER.*)*

MARLENE. Eller, what on Earth? Here, let me help you. Eller, are you alright? Here, sit down.

(ELLER *sits on the bench, holding her head. The* SHER-IFF *enters left.)*

MARLENE. Eller, you've got quite a lump there.

SHERIFF. What's going on here?

MARGIE. For some reason Eller was on the ground behind one of these benches.

SHERIFF. Is this why I haven't been able to find you, because you've been sleeping in the park?

MARLENE. Cole! What an insensitive thing to say. She's got a knot on her head the size of a walnut.

DEPUTY ELLER. *(Pulling off her badge.)* Sheriff, I am tendering my resignation.

SHERIFF. I take it back. Forget I said anything about sleeping on the job.

DEPUTY ELLER. That's not why I am resigning. I've just had an encounter with those Martian boys, and it was too close. They started to transform.

MARGIE. Tom and Hank?

JESS. My Tom and Hank?

MARGIE. *My* Tom, *your* Hank.

JESS. They're not from Mars. I've been working with them for six months.

SHERIFF. *(To* ELLER.*)* What do you mean they started to transform?

(ELLER *re-enacts their transformation act.)*

MARGIE. You mean they turned into monsters? You saw

them do that? Shoot, I was thinking of running off with Tom. If he's a monster –

**DEPUTY ELLER.** They almost transformed, but not exactly.

**SHERIFF.** They did or they didn't? Have you been into Nestor's moonshine?

**DEPUTY ELLER.** No, I have not.

*(Offstage we hear a megaphone.)*

**MAYOR.** *(Offstage.)* Attention, attention. Citizens of Misty Valley, meet in the park A.S.A.P.

**SHERIFF.** Now what?

**MARLENE.** It's Mayor Rushton.

*(The **MAYOR, JUNE, ANDY, LILY, RAINEY, LESTER, NESTOR, MISS PARSONS,** and all citizens and extras enter from all entrances. The **MAYOR** steps up onto the gazebo.)*

**MAYOR.** The Martians have broken in to Wilson's feed store. The whole front is smashed in like it was paper.

**DEPUTY ELLER.** It's those Martian boys again, I'll bet you anything.

**MARLENE.** Was anyone hurt?

**MAYOR.** I don't think so. Wilson was in the basement with his family.

**SHERIFF.** What would Martians want in a feed store?

**MAYOR.** Peanuts.

**MARLENE.** Did you say peanuts?

**MAYOR.** Every bag was ripped into. There are peanut shells everywhere.

**SHERIFF.** I may not know much about intelligent life on other planets, but I can't imagine flying half way across the solar system for peanuts.

**MAYOR.** All I know is, if they'll go to that much trouble for peanuts, then our lives mean nothing to them. We've got to organize a resistance.

*(**WIDOW O'DELL** rushes on left.)*

**WIDOW O'DELL.** Sheriff, sheriff!

**SHERIFF.** Who's calling to me?

**JUNE.** It's Widow O'Dell.

**WIDOW O'DELL.** Sheriff, something awful has happened.

**SHERIFF.** It's been one of those nights.

**WIDOW O'DELL.** Someone shot and killed my poor Bessie.

**ANDY.** Uh-oh.

**MARLENE.** Your prized Holstein is dead?

**WIDOW O'DELL.** She's lying in the middle of the road deader than a door nail. Further up the road is a car smashed into a light pole.

**SHERIFF.** That would explain the power outage.

**WIDOW O'DELL.** Who gives a-gosh-darn about the power going out? What are you going to do about my cow?

**SHERIFF.** Right now I don't know what I can do, other than to put some flares around the remains.

**WIDOW O'DELL.** *(Choking up.)* The remains?

**SHERIFF.** I think that's all we can do for the time being.

**MARLENE.** You don't think that wrecked car hit Bessie, do you?

**WIDOW O'DELL.** No.

**DEPUTY ELLER.** It might have been the Martians.

**WIDOW O'DELL.** It wasn't Martians. I've seen enough bird-shot in my life to know what kind of hole a shotgun makes. You think Martians carry shotguns?

**MAYOR.** I don't know, they like peanuts.

**DEPUTY ELLER.** It was just a thought.

**WIDOW O'DELL.** Eller, if thinking were a bank account, you'd be overdrawn.

(**TOM** *and* **HANK** *run on left.*)

**DEPUTY ELLER.** There they are, the Martians!

(**MARGIE** *runs to stand beside* **TOM**.)

**TOM.** Sheriff, we're not Martians. You've got to believe us.

**DEPUTY ELLER.** Don't listen to them, Sheriff. They could

transform any moment.

**TOM.** We were just making fun.

**DEPUTY ELLER.** I wouldn't trust you varmints any further than I could throw you.

**SHERIFF.** You boys have some explaining to do.

**HANK.** We were just trying to mind our own business, and suddenly we were arrested for being burglars and then accused of being Martians. You can't blame us for trying to get away.

**TOM.** But there is something out there.

**DEPUTY ELLER.** There is?

**TOM.** We heard something on our way down to the station. That's why we turned around and came back here.

**MAYOR.** The whole country is under attack. I say we make a stand. We stand together, or we go down as cowards.

**SHERIFF.** Once and for all, there are no Martians!

(*Sound: something heavy is heard moving through the trees and bushes.*)

**LILY.** Then what's that?

(**LILY** *points toward the audience. Terrified, everyone looks to where* **LILY** *is pointing.*)

**RAINEY.** There in the trees.

**JUNE.** It's coming toward us.

**MARGIE.** I'm scared.

(**MARLENE** *puts her arm* **MARGIE'S** *shoulder. The* **SHER- IFF** *moves closer to the both protectively.*)

**DEPUTY ELLER.** It's a Martian all right, it's got to be.

**MISS PARSONS.** How many? Just one?

**LESTER.** The news says they're all over the place.

**NESTOR.** Hundreds. Thousands. Millions.

**MAYOR.** Get your weapons ready.

**MISS PARSONS.** It's Armageddon. The end has surely come.

**MAYOR.** Stand your ground.

**LILY.** Here it comes. Look at the size of that thing.

**MAYOR.** On my count. One – two –

**MISS PARSONS.** It's. It's.

**SHERIFF.** It's an elephant. Hold your fire.

**MAYOR.** What the – ?

**MISS PARSONS.** Are you sure that's not a tentacle with an eye in it?

**SHERIFF.** Of course, I'm sure. What is an elephant doing in the middle of Misty Valley?

**JESS.** (*Stepping forward so* **HANK** *sees her for the first time.*) I can explain that.

**HANK.** Jess?

**JESS.** Hi, Hank.

**HANK.** Is it really you?

**JESS.** It's me.

**HANK.** You look –

**JESS.** Like a girl?

**HANK.** You took the words right out of my mouth.

**SHERIFF.** Excuse me, young lady. Do you know something about that elephant?

**JESS.** Yes, sir. I'm Jessie Rowley, from the circus train. That is Bonny. I'm her handler. I let her off the train to feed and exercise her, when some wild man showed up screaming something about space monsters and shot two big holes in the water tower. I got drenched, the station flooded, and Bonny got so scared she ran off.

**SHERIFF.** A wild man you say?

**JESS.** Yes.

**SHERIFF.** Can you describe him?

**JESS.** I don't need to, that's him standing right there. (*Points to Nestor.*)

(*An extra enters, pulls the* **MAYOR** *aside, and begins an animated conversation in pantomime.*)

**SHERIFF.** Nestor Pickens, I need a word with you.

**NESTOR.** Sorry, sheriff, I have a train to catch.

**WIDOW O'DELL.** (*Crossing to* **NESTOR.**) You stay right where you are. Are you the maniac who shot my cow?

**NESTOR.** I'm taking the fifth.

**WIDOW O'DELL.** I don't care if you take a gallon. You're paying for my cow.

**SHERIFF.** Not to mention a light pole and the water tower at the station.

**DEPUTY ELLER.** What about the Martians?

**MAYOR.** Well, I declare. There are no Martians. Never was.

(*General stir and ad libs.*)

**MAYOR.** It seems that while the power was out, the rest of the country learned it was just a radio drama by that young upstart Orson Welles.

**DEPUTY ELLER.** That boy is just a flash in the pan. Tomorrow he'll be yesterday's news.

**MAYOR.** It's all over. Everyone can go home.

(*A few of the extras begin to leave.*)

**JESS.** I need to get Bonny back to the train.

**HANK.** I'll go with you.

**JESS.** Why thank you, Hank. (*To* **MARGIE.**) Thanks for everything.

**MARGIE.** (*Hugs* **JESS.**) I'm keeping my fingers crossed.

**HANK.** (*To* **SHERIFF.**) One more thing, Sheriff. About that wall.

**SHERIFF.** It all begins to make sense now. Lucky for you boys we were planning on doing some renovations anyway. Jess and Bonny just started on it a little early.

(**HANK** *shakes hands with the* **SHERIFF** *and he and* **JESS** *exit left.*)

**MISS PARSONS.** I've tolerated as much of this silliness as I intend to. I'll expect to see everyone at Wednesday meeting.

**ANDY.** Silliness? So you knew all along this was a hoax, just like you knew Charlie McCarthy was a dummy.

**MISS PARSONS.** Of course I did. There's no such thing as

space monsters.

*(Sound: we hear the sound of Bonny suddenly trumpeting. **MISS PARSONS** screams and runs off right. Everyone laughs. Sound: Train whistle.)*

**TOM.** That's the fifteen minute warning.

*(**MARGIE** hugs the **SHERIFF** and **MARLENE.**)*

**SHERIFF.** Tom, I expect you to be a gentleman.

**TOM.** You have my word, sir. *(To **MARGIE.**)* Are you ready?

**MARGIE.** *(Suddenly hesitant.)* I can't do this. Not now. I know tonight wasn't real, but for a time it sure felt like it. And it's made me realize how easy it would be to lose everything I have known and loved. I'm not ready to say goodbye to that yet. Maybe in a few months, but not now.

**TOM.** I understand. We'll be coming through this way again.

**SHERIFF.** See you, Tom.

**TOM.** Sir.

**DEPUTY ELLER.** Excuse me, but there's that little matter of the remains under the wall. I have the coroner with me.

**SHERIFF.** Eller.

**DEPUTY ELLER.** I'm sorry, Sheriff, but justice cannot be ignored. Coroner, if you please.

**CORONER.** After a very careful analysis of the tissue found beneath the wall, I have made a positive identification. *(Pause for effect.)* It's meatloaf, Marlene's finest.

*(Cheers and applause. **TOM** hugs **MARGIE** and waves goodbye, exiting left. The crowd disperses. **MARGIE** has her arms around **MARLENE** and her father. As the stage empties, only **ANDY** and **JUNE** are left, holding hands.)*

**JUNE.** It does make you think, doesn't it?

**ANDY.** You mean if the threat had been real?

**JUNE.** It makes you wonder what folks will do in a time of crisis.

**ANDY.** They'll know.

**JUNE.** *(Looking up at the sky.)* Despite everything, it's still
beautiful, isn't it?

**ANDY.** Yes, you are.

**JUNE.** Are you going to ask if you can kiss me?

**ANDY.** You said you're not that kind of girl.

**JUNE.** I keep thinking about what you said if it all came to
an end tonight. I might change my mind.

**ANDY.** You might. When will that be?

> *(***JUNE*** looks up at the stars once more and then turns to*
> **ANDY.** *She takes his other hand in hers. They face each*
> *other.)*

**JUNE.** In about – five seconds.

> *(***JUNE** *and* **ANDY** *move slowly closer, but the lights fade*
> *before we are able to see the kiss.)*

> *(In the dark:)*

**RADIO ANNOUNCER.** It is providence to see couples walking to and fro among the flower beds in the parks, to
hear the laughter of children playing once again, and
to know that in the larger design of the universe this
invasion from Mars is not without its ultimate benefit
for humankind.


**THE END**

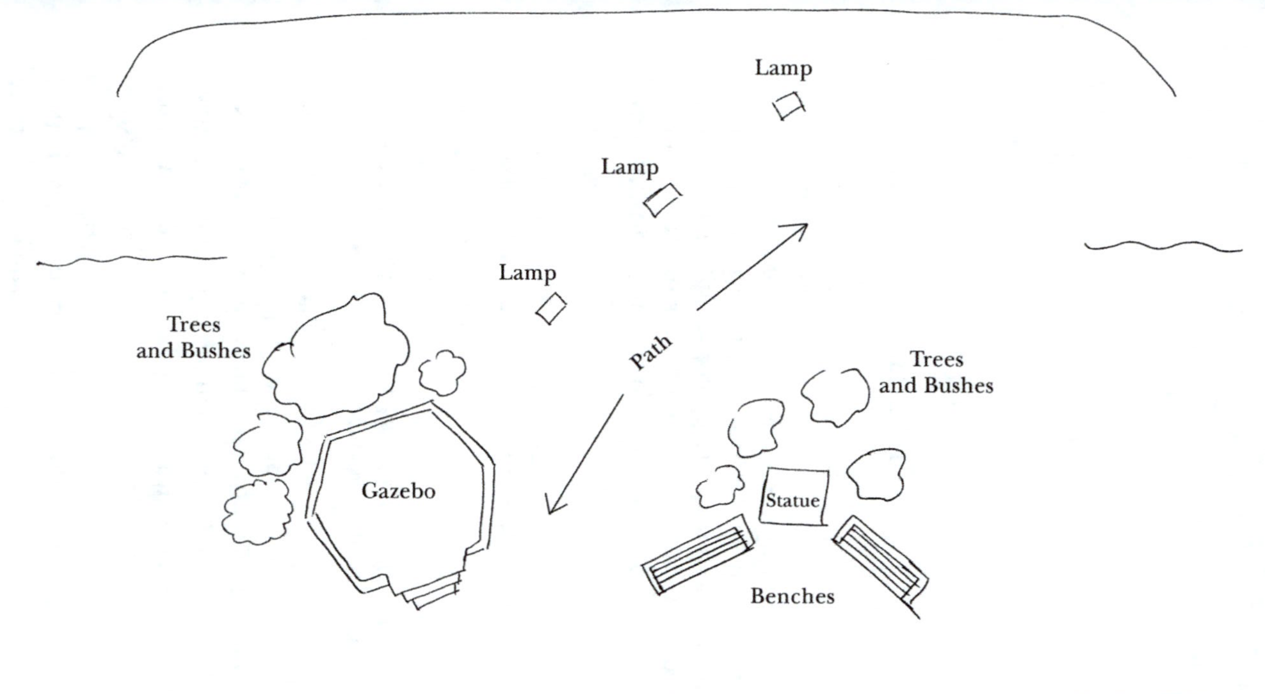


The Panic Broadcast of 1938

If you have enjoyed this publication, you may be interested to know of Jeff Wayne's Musical Version of the *War of The Worlds,* the double album which has sold more than 15 million copies worldwide, as part of Sony BMG's catalogue, and which is now touring the world as a sell-out Multimedia Arena production.

Come see us at: www.thewaroftheworlds.com.

# The Committee Meeting

*A Comedy for Five Women in One Act*
By Joellen K. Bland

*5f / interior*
Sue and her committee get together to plan the church congregational dinner-meeting. While she tries to guide the discussion - often with the aid of a whistle to restore order - Amy prattles, Edith complains, Doris preaches and Mary amiably agrees with just about everything. They willingly offer comments, ideas and suggestions, but when they are asked to assume responsibility, each responds with a prompt excuse for not accepting, and volunteers the time and services of someone else.

Please visit our website **bakersplays.com** for complete descriptions and licensing information

# The Babysitter

*Laurie Woodward 5f / interior*

**Eyes at the window," warns the Ouija board, and Karen realizes that she and her friends are being watched! Searching the house, she discovers there is no child to babysit! An old newspaper clipping reveals that the Williams' baby daughter died mysteriously ten years ago. The terrifying finale reveals who the Williams are, and what is in store for the babysitter! A thriller for all lovers of things that go bump in the night!**

Please visit our website **bakersplays.com** for complete descriptions and licensing information